Spectacular Sports

# Hockey

Counting

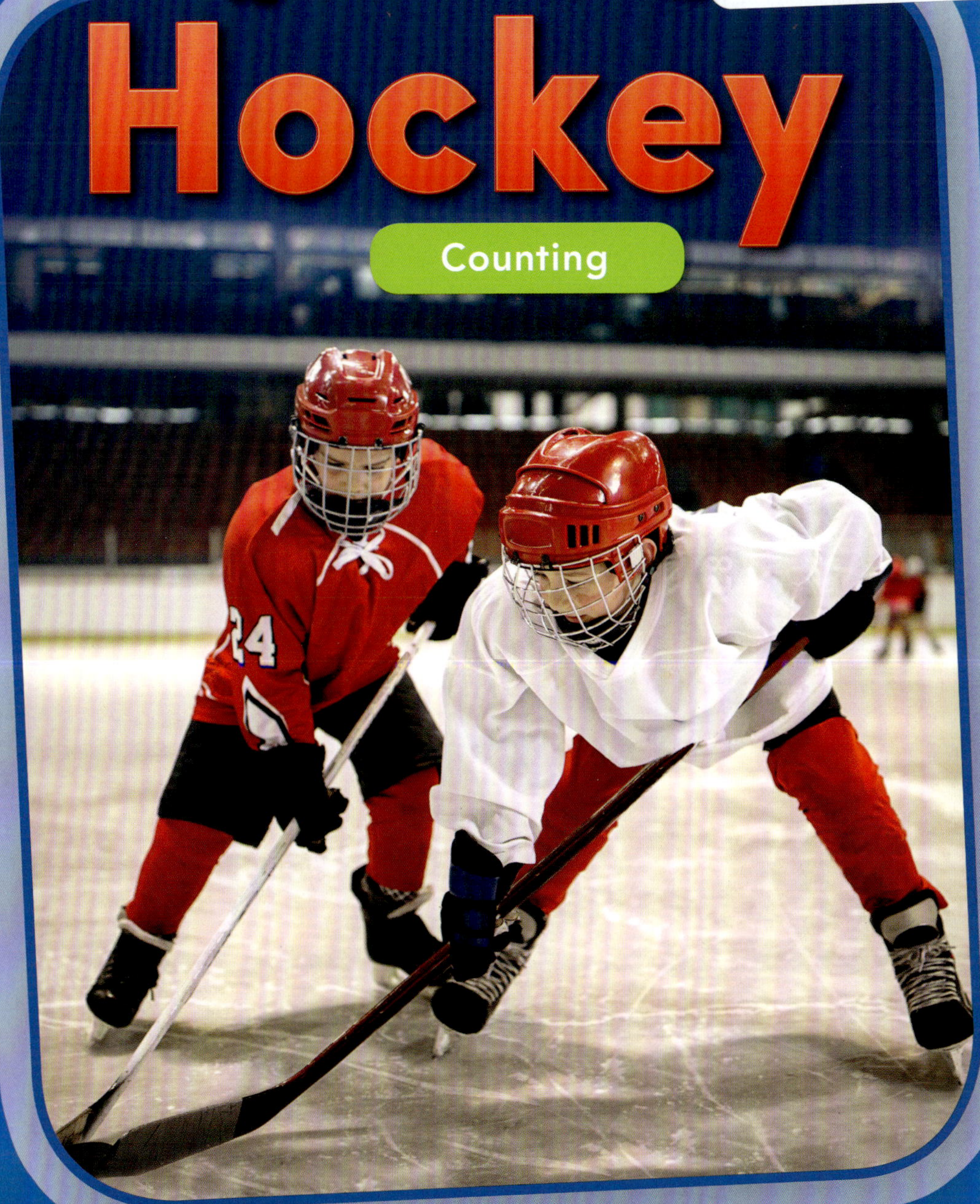

Linda Claire

How many pucks?

# 7

How many nets?

2

How many sticks?

# 13

How many players?

# 12

How many gloves?

# 16

How many skates?

# 10

How many helmets?

# 20

## Problem Solving

Hockey players wear a lot of gear to stay safe. Count the gear and write the numbers.

| | gear | How many? |
|---|---|---|
| 1. |  | |
| 2. | 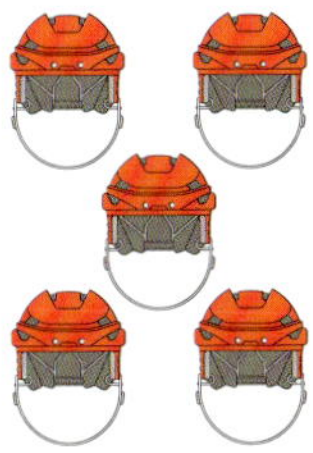 | |
| 3. |  | |
| 4. |  | |

# Answer Key

1. 3 

2. 5 

3. 12 

4. 17 

# Consultants

**Nicole Belasco, M.Ed.**
Kindergarten Teacher, Colonial School District

**Colleen Pollitt, M.A.Ed.**
Math Support Teacher, Howard County Public Schools

**Publishing Credits**

Rachelle Cracchiolo, M.S.Ed., *Publisher*
Conni Medina, M.A.Ed., *Managing Editor*
Dona Herweck Rice, *Series Developer*
Emily R. Smith, M.A.Ed., *Series Developer*
Diana Kenney, M.A.Ed., NBCT, *Content Director*
June Kikuchi, *Content Director*
Véronique Bos, *Creative Director*
Robin Erickson, *Art Director*
Stacy Monsman, M.A., and Karen Malaska, M.Ed., *Editors*
Michelle Jovin, M.A., *Associate Editor*
Fabiola Sepulveda, *Graphic Designer*

**Image Credits:** pp.18–19 Urii Osadch/Shutterstock; all other images from iStock and/or Shutterstock.

**Library of Congress Cataloging-in-Publication Data**

Names: Claire, Linda author.
Title: Spectacular sports. Hockey / Linda Claire.
Other titles: Hockey
Description: Huntington Beach, California : Teacher Created Materials, [2018] | Audience: Grades: K to Grade 3.
Identifiers: LCCN 2017059685 (print) | LCCN 2018021361 (ebook) | ISBN 9781480759503 (e-book) | ISBN 9781425856120 (Paperback)
Subjects: LCSH: Hockey--Juvenile literature. | Counting--Juvenile literature.
Classification: LCC GV847.25 (ebook) | LCC GV847.25 .C47 2018 (print) | DDC 796.962--dc23
LC record available at https://lccn.loc.gov/2017059685

**Teacher Created Materials**
5301 Oceanus Drive
Huntington Beach, CA 92649-1030
www.tcmpub.com

**ISBN 978-1-4258-5612-0**

Printed in China
51497